茂學・峰雋

學生作品集

二零二三

佛教茂峰法師紀念中學

MAU FUNG MEMORIAL COLLEGE BUDDHIST

書　　　　名	《茂學‧峰雋 二零二三》
編　　　　輯	《茂學‧峰雋 二零二三》編輯委員會
出　　　　版	佛教茂峰法師紀念中學
封 面 設 計	5D 吳嘉璇
製　　　　作	超媒體出版有限公司
地　　　　址	荃灣柴灣角街34-36號萬達來工業中心21樓2室
出版計劃查詢	（852）3596 4296
電　　　　郵	info@easy-publish.org
網　　　　址	http://www.easy-publish.org
香 港 總 經 銷	聯合新零售(香港)有限公司
版　　　　次	二零二三年九月初版
圖 書 分 類	流行讀物
國 際 書 號	978-988-8839-44-5
定　　　　價	HK$68

Printed and Published in Hong Kong

序

　　我校一向秉承「明智顯悲」校訓，推行佛化教育，啟發同學智慧，培育善良及慈悲之心，並貫徹優良的關愛文化及卓越的訓輔教育，讓同學在關愛校園環境下愉快學習，透過師生之間互敬互愛的氛圍，培養良好品格和正確的價值觀。

創建才能，發揮所長

教品勵學，熱誠關愛

　　「學習、育才、展能」是學校重要的功能，故我校專注於讓同學在不同的平台發掘、創造及建構才能，發揮一己之長，把握發光發亮的機會，展現豐碩的學習成果。我校老師更無一不致力於努力育才樹人，為我們莘莘學子提供最適切的教育，因材施教，並專注於培養同學高尚的品德情操及正確的道德觀、是非觀。

多元學習，成就人才

　　提供多元化的學習途徑及各種機遇，為自己未來能踏上青雲路而付出努力汗水，亦為社會造就明日棟樑。同學除了能成就一己事業，擁有廣闊的世界視野，亦能惠及社群，心繫家國，將來成為良好的國民。通過中學生涯六年的學習時光，相信同學定能得享「明智成己業，顯悲惠社群；心繫家國情，胸懷世界觀。」的教學成果。

　　《茂學·峰雋　二零二三》收錄了我校近年學生優秀的英文、中文寫作及視覺藝術科作品,為學生創造「展能」的平台,盡展所長,讓同學之間砥礪切磋,見賢思齊,並藉此表揚學生傑出的表現。同時,更希望與各位分享同學的作品、創作的心路歷程及喜悅,我校深信各位的支持及鼓勵將會是同學們尋求進步、精益求精的力量,敬希得到各位的鼎力支持。

　　時光荏苒,盛事如約,本年度適逢我校二十五周年銀禧紀念,感謝各位的信賴,共同見證我們不斷與時代共進,堅定前行,風雨兼程,並贈予諸位我校銀禧周年對聯:

　　　　茂苑興學　　育人明智躍銀禧

　　　　峰雋成才　　律己顯慈惠社群

目錄

目錄 |

樂韻賢聚

視藝科

目錄

那是我吃過最美味的湯圓

1C 林偉杰

今日，是元宵節，我一個人回到宿舍，拿著一份湯圓，坐在那鏽跡斑斑的凳子上吃湯圓。看著外面燦爛的煙花，不禁想起幾年前那一碗我吃過最美味的湯圓。

當年，我才上中一，我認識了一位同學，名叫佳旗，是我的同班同學。我們一開始關係一般，後來每逢數學課，他都會主動幫助我解題，也就從這時開始我們結成好友。放學時，佳旗會問我去不去打球；假期時，我又問他要不要買東西，我們的關係親如手足，形影不離。

有一天，元宵節到了，我跟佳旗說：「我們去買兩份湯圓吧！」佳旗搖搖頭説：「外面的湯圓又貴又不好吃，倒不如我們動手做吧！」聽到這個主意，我不禁連聲説好，於是兩個一胖一瘦的孩子在熱鬧的大街上去買湯圓材料。

買齊材料後，我們回到宿舍做湯圓。因為我們是第一次做，我們只好笨手笨腳地做起來。佳旗僅看了一遍教程，就可以做出小巧玲瓏的湯圓。湯圓圓圓的，像十五的滿月，模樣如小核桃那麼大，白白嫩嫩的，我滿是羨慕。佳旗看著我的湯圓，外表奇奇

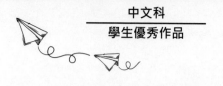

怪怪，黑芝麻的餡都露了出來。他笑著説：「我父母是做麵粉的，所以我也會一點，我來教你吧！」每當我有不解的時候，他都仔細跟我解釋，還鼓勵我，看著他堅定的眼神，我心頭暖暖的。

經過我們一番努力，我們終於包好所有湯圓，當時已是半夜，我們還沒煮湯圓就睡了。清涼的晨風吹拂著我的臉，把我們弄醒。身旁的佳旗説道：「湯圓已煮好，快日出了，我們不如一邊看日出，一邊嚐湯圓，好嗎？」我們跑到宿舍的露台，坐在那鏽跡斑斑的凳子上，我夾起一個湯圓送到嘴裡，香甜酥糯，滿口留香，黑芝麻的香味深深地陷入我的味蕾。我笑了，佳旗也笑了，我們不約而同地説：「那是我吃過最美味的湯圓。」那金燦燦而又溫暖的陽光灑在我們身上，我感到前所未有的溫暖。當時我們還約定明年的元宵節再做湯圓，但元宵節未到他就已經轉學了。

如今，我已上中四了，雖然每年元宵節我也嚐過很多湯圓，但都不及我們親手做的湯圓好吃。此時，我的視線模糊了眼前手中的那碗湯圓，那一胖一瘦的孩子在熱鬧的大街上的身影，又在我腦海浮現，每當想起他時，我的眼淚又禁不住流下。

> 那又圓又甜的湯圓味道，叫人至今難忘，難忘的不僅是味覺上的甜味，而且是生活的甜味。成長路上，有幸遇到良朋益友，伴我在陡峭的人生路前行。朋友一個肯定的眼神、一句鼓勵的說話、一個溫暖的擁抱，實在是微小而確實的美好，並一一在我心中播下友情的種子，縱然大家天各一方，但那友情之花仍是燦爛地盛開。

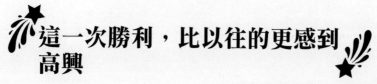

這一次勝利，比以往的更感到高興

2C 曾俊博

集體的榮譽難道比個人的榮譽更好嗎？以往的我，在羽毛球賽場上單打「十勝無一輸」，而在某一場比賽，教練突然安排我和一個素未謀面的隊友一同雙打，我只好無奈接受。

比賽前，我們訓練了一整天，效果怎麼說呢？十全十美卻又美中不足。這句話看起來是互相矛盾的，可是事實就是這樣。因為長期單打的我過於注重個人的實力表現而輕視團隊合作，目中無人，認為即使沒有隊友，自己獨自比賽也可以輕易奪冠。

正因為自己的自大、驕傲和急於表現自己的能力，所以不慎在比賽中誤傷隊友，導致比賽被迫中斷，最終草草作罷。隨後，我看著被圍得水泄不通的人群中，坐著一個滿頭是血還在嚎叫的隊友。我也不知道怎麼的，便默默地走向休息室，坐到椅子上。

突然，我彷彿被一股無形的力量拉到一個別人看不見的空間。「他們」在批判我，在指責我。我開始反思起來……

　　若是我沒有那麼自大，願意多和隊友溝通，訓練時互相配合，是不是就不會發生今天這件事？我後悔莫及，卻暗自下定決心：從今往後，不管是甚麼形式的比賽，都應被重視對待。

　　思緒忽爾被拉回現實，如今的我不再如以往那個自大的我了。我開始認真和隊友一同訓練，互相配合，積極投入比賽當中和隊友成了無話不說的伙伴。

　　我本以為自那次意外以後，隊友會疏遠我，沒想到他養傷回來後，只是對我笑笑話：「沒事！」幸好有隊友的不計前嫌，我和他配合得越來越好，屢屢一同摘下羽毛球雙打冠軍。這一刻，我倆牽手站上頒獎台上，我們相視而笑，我心裡想著：「這一次勝利，比以往的更感到高興！」

　　集體的榮譽難道比個人的榮譽更好嗎？其實不然，兩者是無法比較的，它們是相互的。每個人只有融入到集體中才會有更大的成就，帶來的幸福感與滿足感才會更多，更深刻，更難忘，這才是一個真正的團體之存在意義。

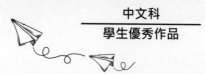

> 通往成功的途徑五花八門，一個人的成功是成功，難道承載眾人汗水的成功果實就不能算是成功嗎？豐富自己內涵，改變自己的狹隘心胸，接受與他人同行，腳踏實地，不急於求成，也不再固執堅持個人主義，不難發現「條條大路通羅馬」所帶來的喜悅感。

這一次勝利，比以往的更有意義

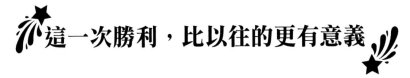

2D 陳盈茵

　　猶記得五年前的今天，我站在頒獎台看著台下的觀眾，心裡十分淡然，因為我知道這個榮耀不是靠自己得來的。

　　可是，我的老師在台下高興萬分，因為他正為自己的學生獲獎而感到無比興奮，然而老師看著我目無表情的模樣，不禁生氣地說：「快笑一笑！觀眾們在看著你呢！」望著台下觀眾熱切的眼神，我卻苦笑一下。

　　回到現在，我到達了比賽現場，老師跟我說：「一定要依我話去做！一定要，不然我不讓你參加任何比賽了！」那反覆的叮嚀及斬釘截鐵的命令，彷彿叫我不得不遵循，可是我不知從何來的勇氣，心想：「我今次就會不聽他的話，我要嘗試根據自己的靈感和技術去畫出屬於自己的作品！」

　　在我認真作畫的時候，我的老師在台下瘋狂小聲地提醒我，要跟著他的指示去做，我卻連正眼都沒看他，只埋首自己的創作。我的漠視終於激怒了老師，他憤怒地喝令我：「依我的話去做！你有沒有聽到我說話嗎？」我還是沒理他，他更顯得不耐煩地說：「你

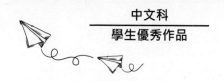

再不理我，我就不准你報名比賽，更莫説要參加畫展了！」儘管參加畫展是我日思夜想的夢想，我仍膽大地向他做了一個鬼面。他氣瘋了，在台下瘋狂瞪著我。

　　最後，在我熟練的技術和充滿創意的靈感下，我最終得到了這場比賽的冠軍。評判邀請我上台發表獲獎感言，我決意要表達真正的感言，而不是那虛假的劇本。我昂然地對台下的觀眾説：「從前的我不是真正的我，以往的我只是跟著劇本的機械人，沒有自我意識、沒有創作的靈魂、沒有創意的發揮。我現在自豪地跟大家説，從這次比賽中，我明白到作畫的真諦，我終於能在創作的天空上自由地飛翔。」説罷台下響起此起彼落的掌聲及歡呼聲，人們紛紛拍掌欣賞我，欣賞我可以把現實中的「我」喚醒。

　　這一次勝利，比以往更有意義呢！

　　創作的天地無邊無垠，能夠發揮心中的創意，跳出模仿的框架，締造無限的可能，實在是一件愉悦的美事，再者能夠得到大家的肯定和認同，相信更為創作的力量注入強心針，這的確是別具意義的勝利！

您是我的好榜樣，在您身上我學會了甚麼是正語

3E 陳熹洋

　　語言，可以用來鼓勵人，令他人歡喜；也可以用來傷害人，令他人痛苦。雖然我們每一個正常的人一出生就被賦予說話的能力，但是很多時候一些不當的言語還是會一不小心傷害到別人。所以即使是簡單的說話，也需要運用技巧才能好好地與人溝通。

　　「快遲到了，可否快點！」聲音在房中迴旋，煩躁的我在家門口跺腳等待，等待媽媽一起出門。片刻後媽媽終於走到門前說：「可以出門了。」又問我：「東西帶齊了嗎？」正因剛才的事，煩躁的我在發脾氣，不想理會她，一心想盡快趕去活動的地方。在路上我一直跑，媽媽在後面一直追，就快連我的影子都看不見了。排隊上車時，剎那間，我發現我竟把手機忘記在家中！我皺著眉頭轉身望向媽媽，原以為她會反過來抱怨我丟三落四，還要一直催促她，怎料她只是以平和的語氣對我說：「那你快回去拿吧，我在這兒等你，要小心啊！」我呆滯了一秒，便飛快地往回跑了。路上我有點感動，但同時也帶有點歉意及慚愧，我剛才的話是不是有點過分了呢？為何明明是兩件類似的事，但帶給人的感覺像是截然不同的呢？

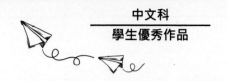
　　每個人都會犯錯，小孩子更是。但在我們家，每當我犯錯或是未如理想時，媽媽都會鼓勵而不是指責我為何未能達到要求。例如：當我考試未如理想時媽媽會說：「沒事，下次努力，我相信你！」即使在我考試考得好時，媽媽更會大方地讚賞我及鼓勵我繼續前進。媽媽說出來的話是有魔力的，每一句都能說得精準及合適，令相互都快樂。由此，我感受到每個人說話的不同層次，真的會有不同結果。

　　走在大街上，可能不時便會聽到一些不好的言語一連串地噴出來。路上的行人仿似已習以為常，是他們都認同嗎？不是，誰都不想聽，但那又如何呢？快速及不經大腦的言語帶給那人快感，但他卻忘記了別人的感受。在佛教中常說的業便由此招來。

　　在佛教的八正道中，有「正語」這一門戒學。「正語」簡單來說就是正確的言語，即是說出來的話真實不虛、不會傷害到別人及能夠幫助到人，即使遇到惡言惡語的人，我們亦應多加包容與諒解，不以惡語回敬對方。

　　媽媽，您是我的好榜樣，在您身上我學會了甚麼是「正語」。

　　簡單的說話可以簡單地隨口而出，但我們說的每一句話都應經過思考再而作出行動。

> 我們每人每天平均會說 800 至 1400 個字。說話是一門學問，要讓每一句、每一字表達的意思正確無誤並不容易，說話時要同時留意自己的言語是否恰當，更是不易。語言能鼓勵別人，表達愛意，同時也能傷害別人。在佛學課上，當說到八正道的「正語」時，我想起自己平時的不當言辭，讓我深深反省，最後便造就了這篇文章。

「那天，我學會甚麼是無常……」

3E 賴佳蔚

那天，我學會甚麼是無常。我明白到生離死別是沒有人能逃避的事。我們應該體會無常，積極創造因緣，好好善待、珍惜每個相遇的人，廣結善緣，把握當下，放下我執，坦然地面對人生。

一年前的一天，奶奶突然病倒了，令我和爸媽都措手不及。在那個夜晚，外面狂風暴雨，我看著父母心急如焚地把奶奶送到救護車上，我心裏默默祈禱，希望奶奶千萬不要出事！我坐在急救室門外，氣氛詭異的安靜，我緩緩閉上雙眸，腦中浮現的是與祖母相處的一點一滴。

記得小時候回家鄉時，奶奶常常坐在菩提樹下的石凳，而我會坐在她的旁邊，輕靠着她那健壯的肩膀。有時，奶奶會慢慢地唸一首古詩；有時，奶奶輕柔地哼唱一支動聽的民謠；有時，奶奶會跟我說一個意味深長的寓言故事。記得奶奶常常說：「人生無常，世事難料。既來之，則安之。」那時的我對這句話一竅不通，或許是因為我年紀還太小。奶奶常常說：「你長大後，就會明白我說的話，這樣你的人生就不會感到那麼痛苦！」那時候的我，總以為昨天如此，今天如此，明天也必定如此，我以為跟奶奶美好的相處時光，永遠不會改變。但事與願違，明天不一定會如常來

臨，沒有事物是永恆不變的，生離死別，是沒有人能逃避的事。

不知沉思了多久，我聽到爸爸緩緩地說：「醫生說我們可以進去了！」我那飄遠的思緒回來了。推開眼前無比沉重的房門後，映入眼簾的是一片的蒼白。我不敢相信躺在病床上的人就是奶奶。以前奶奶的眼睛炯炯有神，臉色紅潤。現在奶奶變得陌生了，她躺在床上一動不動，變成了冷冰冰的屍體。我鼻子一酸，淚水在眼裡不斷打轉，最後淚水還是劃過我那目無表情的臉頰。

一剎那，我仿佛明白了奶奶那句話。我緩緩開口說：「人生無常，世事難料。」我終於明白了奶奶這句話，原來奶奶告訴我世事無常，就如現在，奶奶突然離世，就是無常。我慣性地誤以為萬物是「有常」的，因此，當事情出現變化，就會難以接受，進而感到痛苦。原來世間一切事物，都在不斷變化，並非所有事情都能由自己主宰。奶奶的事令我深刻地體驗到「無常」。

我對著眼前的奶奶說：「我明白了！」但她早已永遠閉上了雙眸。雨，終於停了。現在一條五顏六色的彩虹，高高掛在蔚藍的天空中。爸媽站在病床前，宛若兩個孩童般嚎啕大哭。我用紙巾擦拭他們臉頰上的眼淚，輕聲地安慰著他們，只因我認識了「無常」，知道他們正是我要珍惜一生的人。

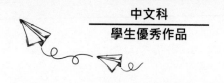

　　我明白了，人生變幻無常，世間一切如同泡沫，變化不定，亦虛亦幻。佛法所言，人生是眾緣和合才出現，因緣條件改變而即逝。面對著變幻莫測的人生，我們常常感到無奈與無助，我們總會在大喜大悲中無所適從。不過，我們只是一個個凡人，無法得知未來是好是壞，人，必須學會隨遇而安。奶奶説得對：「既來之，則安之。」生活就是一場修行，一切事物也有成、住、壞、空，我們要接受人生是無法預測，沒有事物能永恆不變。既然每次相見如此難得，那就要好好珍惜，接受積極活著的無常，重視生命中的每一刻，正如星雲大師所説：「因為無常，才有希望，因為無常，才有未來。」

　　在最初的時候，我對於作文題目「無常」，感到毫無頭緒，不知從何入手。但這時，我想起佛學老師説過無常是指世間的萬物有生有滅，不會永恆不變，亦令我想起親人的離世，自己對此痛苦不已。因此，我以自己的經歷，創作了這篇文章。

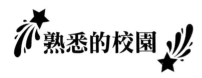
熟悉的校園

4B 蔡偉鋒

那天，我瀏覽社交平台，發現一則難以接受的消息……

小學母校將會被清拆，改建成一家商場。那時我還以為是一則假消息，但在我再三確認之下，我只好面對無奈的現實。

小學被清拆前，我重返到校園的門前。邁着沉重的腳步走進校園，一幕幕的記憶重演眼前，那時候的籃球場、那時候的有蓋操場、那時候的禮堂……我想不到走進這熟悉的校園，當中的一景一物，都勾起了我不同的回憶，撫今追昔，甚至令我百感交集。

我走到操場小賣部前。還記得，每逢小息，小賣部總是人山人海，但現在變得物是人非。那時候，我常與小賣部的阿姨和叔叔閒聊日常。令我印象最深刻的是，那次我遲到了，沒有吃早餐，未吃早餐的我走路乏力，小賣部的阿姨看到，她二話不說，把最後一份三文治遞給我，還說請我吃的。那三文治的味道我至今還記得，但就是那種美味，難以忘懷。突然想到，我還有一件未了的事！只記得畢業那天，我手執畢業證書，跑到小賣部，才發現小賣部沒有營業，我一直未跟阿姨、叔叔好好道一聲「再見」，那是我深藏內心的遺憾。

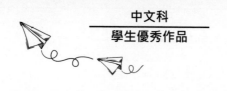

帶着遺憾的我，走到我小時候的噩夢——留堂室。我苦笑一聲，走進去，課室的布置沒有變化，我走向小時候經常坐的那個座位。一位老師令我印象最深刻，那是李老師，我們稱呼她為「百變怪」，因為她的變面速度驚人，上一秒還臉帶微笑，下一秒就想把你吃掉了，所以大家都不敢令她生氣。但我剛好相反，她越生氣，我越頑皮，有時還會頂她的嘴。但是現在回想，才覺得自己那時有多麼傻，她每次罰我、責罵我，令我以後做事做人更加專注細節。在我想得入神時，我看到桌上寫着很多罵李老師的話，那些字不是別人的，而是我的。小時候寫着罵李老師的話，但長大後，才知道李老師為我費盡心思。最後，我補上了幾行大字：「李老師，我長大了，才明白你『愛之深，責之切』的道理，謝謝你！」

我突然很想回到昔日的課室，也想起當時的同學。所以我就跑到課室門前，一打開門，驚訝地看見幾張熟悉而陌生的面孔！我回過神來，他們是我小時候的「死黨」，原來他們也看到那則消息，所以特意回來看一看，大家就如約定好一樣，重返課室，真是奇妙！我們回憶起一起唱校歌、一起朗讀課文、一起在課堂上胡鬧……那些點點滴滴就如昨天發生一樣。那時候，每天總會玩一種遊戲——紙疊球，我們很有默契地點一點頭，立刻動手準備，我們十分熟練地從「老地方」拿出工具，一切準備好，我再次站到投球手的位置，我們彷彿回到小時候，那時我的眼不爭氣地流

出眼淚，歡聲笑語中，我們打完了小學最後一場的紙疊球。

　　到了清拆當天，我眼前的母校變成廢墟，內心百感交集。心裏一直希望只是一場夢，一想到兩天前還在的小學校園一下子沒有了，那椎心的痛令我窒息。以前的我少不更事，臉帶稚氣地戲言：「學校甚麼時候才能拆掉？」但如今，真的要清拆的時候，哽咽的我只能悔不當初……

> 校園內發生的點點滴滴教我難以忘懷。我透過記述各種回憶，抒發當中的感受。我曾讀過一些以校園題材的文章，從中得到了不少靈感，亦應用到本文當中。

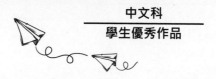

您是我的好榜樣，在您身上我學會了堅持

4D 吳煒軒

　　布達拉宮裏佛像的佛光普照著他們每一個人，他們每一個人都是佛化教育中虔誠的信徒。

　　在崎嶇的川藏公路上有著這麼一群人，他們是虔誠的佛教徒，一心便是其中一員，每走三步向前方行一下跪拜禮，歷經磨難只為到拉薩祈求佛祖普渡眾生，人們尊稱這群人為「朝聖者」。在路人不解的眼神之中，這般奇特的行為也自然融為了川藏公路的一道風景線，他們是我的好榜樣，在他們身上我學到了堅持，不忘初心，一入佛門，一心向佛的信念！

　　崎嶇的山路，陡峭的地形，從四川到拉薩兩千一百公里，一心不為世俗而折服，只為淨化心靈祈求佛祖保佑芸芸眾生。道阻且長，行則將至！晝夜不停、風雨無阻的朝聖之路令他的額頭在磕傷與恢復之間反復拉扯，傷口處結下的血痂便是一路上最好的明證。匍匐下跪五體投地，無人監督卻十分規範，這些樸實無華的動作無不突顯出朝聖者對佛祖的尊敬與謙卑。變化無常的天氣席捲著高原，沙塵暴和雪災相繼而來，一路的虔誠跪拜和惡劣的環境令一心的關節變得腫大，脆弱的皮膚也裂開來。但一心沒有

過多休息，因為他相信朝聖路上的艱辛正是他意志的考驗！

　　西藏也許會缺氧，但從不缺信仰！進入拉薩證明他離心中佛的距離僅剩一千五百公里。高達四千五百米的高原海拔令大多數朝聖者感到不適，但一心沒有選擇退出，他臉上流露出充滿信仰力量的笑容，他的表情仿佛在訴說著佛祖就在前方，驅使他堅持向著前方前進。

　　巔峰守護著每一位前進者，黃昏見證著虔誠的信徒！在黃昏的照耀下，朝聖者們帶著信仰歷時過百天終於到達目的地，黃昏的照耀令一心的臉顯得泛黃，這見證著這一路走來的滄桑與磨煉。兩千一百公里的路途艱辛但從不放棄，即使翻山越嶺也絕不卻步，這些永不言棄的意志是一心向佛的信念，是他對心中佛祖的尊敬。

　　一心並不是因為巔峰而慕名而來，但在眾人信仰科學的時代他仍然堅定信仰。一心是我的好榜樣，在他的故事中，我學到了堅持信念，我明白到當我們身處在逆境之中，心要不受影響，砥礪前行！

中文科
學生優秀作品

在人文紀錄片「朝聖之路」中，我看到了朝聖者在朝聖路上的故事，他們對信仰的堅定和尊敬值得讓人學習。朝聖路上縱然歷練磨難，但內心澄明，沒有受到各種內外因素的束縛，放下所有負面的執著，他們的精神激勵著我在人生路上，堅持信念，向前邁進。

自此之後，我終於解開了心結

5C 何子健

　　每當我打開相簿，看到我和爺爺的合照時，我都為曾經誤會了爺爺感到懊悔。幸好，最後我對爺爺的心結解開了，與爺爺度過了一段愉快的生活。

　　我從小在市區裏跟爸爸媽媽一起生活，可是，好景不長，爸爸媽媽後來因為感情變化，經常吵架，後來，關係日趨惡劣，爺爺看不過眼，於是便獨自帶我到鄉下居住。對此，爸爸媽媽沒有反對，並承諾每月將生活費寄給爺爺，我卻感到無奈萬分，像是被離棄一樣。要跟爺爺到鄉下居住，也非我的意願，全都怪爺爺多管閒事，對此，我感到十分不滿。

　　爺爺的家位處偏僻，交通十分不便。家裡陳設簡陋和單調，沒有電玩、沒有網絡，甚至手機也不能完好地充電。在這裡，悶極了，我沒甚麼事可以做。我討厭爺爺，怪責他為何把我帶來這這裡。每次我發脾氣時，爺爺都只是默不作聲，也沒有向我作任何的解釋。對此，我只好不以為然，獨自生活。

　　由於搬到鄉下地方與爺爺同住，為了方便接送，我也轉到附近的鄉郊學校。跟心裡盤算的一樣，校內的所有東西都已過時，

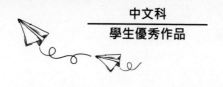
學習的內容我也早已學過了。每天放學，我只有百無聊賴地四處遊逛，不喜歡回到爺爺老舊的住處。除了吃晚飯時間，我幾乎都在外留連。即使回到家裡，我也刻意跟爺爺作對，把書包隨意丟到一角，爺爺見狀，每次只是默默地拾起來。吃飯的時候，爺爺也會問我學校的情況，我每次也只是淡淡的回應。

後來，我漸漸明白，爺爺獨力照顧我，也是一件苦事，可是我仍埋怨爺爺擅自把我帶到鄉下生活，我的心結仍未解開，我仍未能接受爺爺。同時，我也納悶，為何爸爸媽媽不反對，他們雖然偶然會來探望我，但從不提何時接我回去，我想，必定是爺爺怕悶，要我留在這裏陪他，一想到這裡，我的心結更緊了。

時間一天一天過去，我和爺爺的關係沒有太大的變化。由於今天感到疲憊不堪，所以放學後便馬上回家，原本打算直接回房間睡覺。突然間，聽到像是爺爺的嘈吵聲音，由於平常很少聽到，出於好奇，於是去看個究竟。我悄悄躲在門後，爺爺似乎在跟我的爸爸通話，爺爺大吼：「你好意思讓他回去？當我孫子回去，看到那位所謂的新媽媽，我的孫子會怎樣想？你有否考慮孩子的感受？你放心！你們離婚的事，待孫子長大，我會向他交代。我知道孫子現在不太喜歡我，但至少有我照顧他。回到你們處，即使房子再大再漂亮，你們卻沒有關心過他……孫子小小年紀，我不想讓他沒人照顧！我會好好保護他！」聽到這裡，我的心頭一

震，久久不能平復。對於這突如其來的消息，我實在難以接受，這刻百感交集，但對於爺爺的理解，似乎深厚了一些。

經過多番思量後，我對爺爺有著滿滿的歉疚，此時我的心結解開了，淚如雨下，原來最關懷我的是爺爺，我沒有資格恨爺爺，他才是最為我著想的人。我慢慢打開房門，爺爺突然說道：「噢！你回來了，快快出來吃飯。」爺爺看見我滿眼通紅，立刻問道：「怎樣了？哪裡受傷了？身體不適嗎？在學校被同學欺負了嗎？」看到爺爺對我的關切，我再也忍不住，跑到爺爺面前，一把抱著爺爺說：「對不起……爺爺……」爺爺輕輕安慰了我，我跟爺爺表示我明白了一切，所有盡在不言中。

我對爺爺的心結解開了，我的人生有了重大的改變，我跟著爺爺到街口放風箏和四處品嚐鄉下美食。我有空便到鄉下四處走走，我和爺爺一同走過美麗的山和看過寧靜的湖，這裡令我感到舒適，這是我心結解開的地方。

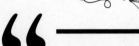

中文科
學生優秀作品

　　文章取材源於一段與爺爺回鄉生活的經歷，主角對於爺爺的態度，由誤解到理解，由拒絕到接受，最後明白原來身旁的爺爺才是對自己最好的人，文章情節起伏多變，張弛有度，寫主角與爺爺的矛盾十分銳利，同時反襯出爺爺默默承受的大愛。最後揭示事件底蘊，令主角猛然醒覺，悔不當初，由是心結解開，明白自己的狂妄與不辛。整體寫來，情節推進甚是流暢，主角與爺爺形象鮮明突出，寫出現今世代人倫關係的脆弱，但同時寄意恪守親情的可貴。

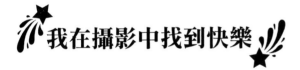

我在攝影中找到快樂

5C 羅嘉宜

有時候，我總在思考，甚麼是快樂？如何可以得到快樂？這是一種情緒嗎？快樂的定義到底是甚麼？直至我投入攝影世界，我相信我找到快樂了。

我自小已與攝影有一段淵源。我的爸爸是一位攝影師，從小到大都會給我們一家大小拍攝很多照片。他會跟我分享拍攝時遇到的趣事。當時，我年紀尚小，總喜歡倚著爸爸，聽他細說各項有關攝影的故事。也許，就是從這個時候開始，埋下了攝影興趣的種子。

後來，攝影手機普及起來，人人都用手機拍攝，我也偶然拍拍鬧著玩。也許我的體內早已存有攝影的基因，拍出來的相片都獲得朋友讚賞，並且在不同的社交媒體流傳。面對同學的誇讚，我也不以為意，當然還沒有真正喜歡攝影。

十五歲生日的前一天，爸爸突然因急病走了，無盡的悲傷伴隨著我整個中學生活。在收拾父親的遺物時，我無意中發現了爸爸的寶物，是一部黑色的尼康菲林相機，外皮有點發霉，但機械菲林轉軸還是很順暢，轉動時會發出「卡卡」的聲音，仿佛呼叫

著我還在的訊息。

拿起相機的一刻，腦海裏想起了很多很多兒時的回憶，那時候，父親幾乎每天都拿著相機四處拍攝。有時候，對著重複的風景不斷地拍，也在不同的時間，專程走去拍。有時候會對我不斷地拍，有時候，還會在我跟姐姐鬧著玩時，靜靜地坐一旁拍。真可以說是機不離手啊！想到這裡，我默默地舉起相機，透過明亮的觀景器重新審視這個世界，近乎本能的完成構圖、操作，在按下快門的瞬間，一絲快樂的感覺頓時油然而生。

鏡頭下的世界是有趣的，看著流動的風景，有朝氣的城市脈搏，熱鬧的節慶活動，不同的紀念日慶祝，甚至偶爾到一些義工機構，幫忙拍攝活動花絮，最美的時刻都被我記錄下來，這一切都是美好的。攝影治癒了我喪父之痛，生活的美好事物，都在我按下快門的一刻被凝固住了。在拍照的時候，我甚至會看到爸爸的模樣，彷彿他還在我身邊，沒有離我而去，就像小時候，用他慈祥的雙手，親自教我如何拍攝。

我從攝影中找到快樂，找到父親的影子，我依著父親的路，拿著相機四處奔走，四處尋訪美景。我與其他人分享相片及拍攝的心路經歷，得到無數的稱讚。爸爸的舊同事看過我的作品後，說我的拍攝風格跟爸爸很相近，有著當年共事的感覺。每當聽到

這些説話時，我不期然感到莫名的自豪，我甚至感到父親一直在我身旁，沒有離開過我，他只是換了一種方式來陪伴和教導我。雖然他不在我身邊，但在我的生活環境裏，總有他的身影。我漸漸明白到，逝者如斯，思念是無處不在，是揮之不去，與其生活在痛苦裡，不如迎來明天，接受自己思念的感覺，讓親人以一種全新的方式與自己生活，這樣的人生會更有意義。

其實使人感到快樂的方法有很多，可以是做自己喜歡的事，可以是浸醉於某一個時刻，可以是停留在某段記憶裡。而我從攝影中找到快樂，找到親人，感到父親永遠與我常在，讓我更會珍惜現在的一切。

> 攝影不單是興趣，更可以連繫人心，縱使陰陽永隔，透過按下快門，逝者與生者恍如又再次活到同一個時空裡。文中細膩描寫主角的感情變化，對於父親的離世，由痛苦無奈，無法自處，到積極面對，勇於接受。一部被擱置多時已被塵封的相機，落到作者手裡隨即添了生機。與之同時，無形的父愛，通過一張張風格類同的相片洋溢展現，寓情於物，運於天成；主角由此找到人生的意義，縱使面對親人離世，亦能勇敢面對，立意積極，甚是可取。

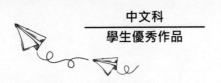

中文科
學生優秀作品

我曾參與一次活動，當中的經歷令我覺醒過來，明白到「己所不欲，勿施於人」的道理

5D 張雲楓

還記得從前我是一個沒有同理心的人。直到那次活動，才讓我明白「己所不欲，勿施於人」的道理。

那年的一個星期六，天氣不怎麼好，雲也是灰黑的，像我的心情一般，談不上開心，因為本是假期的星期六，我卻被老師叫去參加一個活動。聽說是關於讓視力弱甚至看不見的長者體會到人間自有真情在，讓他們知道人間有愛，還是有人在乎他們，而我卻覺得沒用，甚至是多餘！「這些人反正都看不見了，幹甚麼還麻煩我！」我喃喃道。在踏上回校的路上，走到一處紅綠燈時，我還在細聲細語的抱怨。此時，一股清脆的敲擊聲傳來，回首一望，正是一個眼被黑布蒙著，拿著紅白色拐杖的老頭，加上他熟悉的敲打，我斷定他一定是一個瞎子，頓時玩心大起，走到他身後敲他的腦袋一下，然後又走去他的身前……戲弄了好一會，直到看到綠燈亮起我才作罷，在我轉身前他卻面不改色的嗅了一下我衣服的味道，然後問到：「請問你可以扶我過馬路嗎？」我本來就不喜歡瞎子，加上這個活動更是令我反感，又怎麼可能幫你呢？所以我笑了笑便丟下他跑去對面。

中文科
學生優秀作品

　　過了不一會我就到了學校，緊接著就開始活動了。第一個活動就是自己親身體驗盲人的感覺，用黑布把雙眼蒙上，直到這一刻我才發現看不見的恐怖之處，而且竟然要蒙上雙眼一個小時！我頓感大事不妙，果然，最怕甚麼就來甚麼。我要獨自過馬路，由同學扶我到馬路附近，然後他就離開了，只剩下我一個人，我因為什麼都看不見遲遲不敢動身，這種感覺好像在哪裡遇到過，又好像想不起來。此時，忽然有一股飄著花香的香水味傳來，想必一定是個善解人意的大姐姐，我便緩緩開口問道：「可以扶我過馬路嗎？」，沒有得到對方的回應，卻只聽到綠燈「嘟、嘟、嘟」聲響起時那高跟鞋的聲音越來越遠，花香味也消散了。我一開始有些不知所措，緊接著就是憤怒，心裡罵道為甚麼現在的人這麼沒有同理心，盲人過馬路都不幫忙一下，但突然想起早上熟悉的畫面，早上的我對那位老人家的行為，我的怒火瞬間就熄滅了，才意識到自己好像有些不對，有那麼一絲絲的愧疚。

　　我只能狠狠地扶牆走回學校，進行下一個活動。下一項活動居然是獨自吃東西。我抓摸著，好不容易找到一個位置，正要坐下去卻坐了空，直接重重的摔在地上，我聽到了數不盡的嘲笑聲音，卻又無能為力，這時有一位同學扶了我起來，並帶我去其他地方坐下來。她耐心地告訴我食物的位置，在她的幫助下我終於可以吃東西了，這時我才明白，一個看不見的人是多麼無助，多

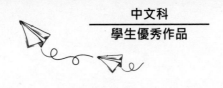

麼需要一雙「眼睛」。這眼睛並不是看東西的眼睛，而是一個幫助他、關心他、在乎他的人。雖然他的眼睛看不見，但他的心卻能「看見」。再一次回想起早上的我，愧疚之心又多了一分，我才明白，做甚麼事都應該代入別人的角度，考慮對方、推己及人、將心比心！

　　最終這個活動也算是順利完成了，最後才開始是次活動的重頭戲。陪伴失明長者幾個小時，經過了親身體驗盲人的感受後，我清楚的知道看不見有多麻煩、多「丟臉」。這時，失明的老人家們都在同學們的攙扶下進入了禮堂，「砰、砰、砰」清脆的敲擊聲響起，只見一個熟悉的人慢慢走來，他眼睛蒙著黑布，手拿著紅白色拐杖，我口張得很大，十分震驚，他貌似也察覺到異樣，問道：「怎麼了？」順帶嗅了一下我衣服的味道，他依舊面不改色的說道：「我不怪你。」看著他面帶微笑，再想起我對這位老人家的所作所為，慚愧之心更深了，隨後我十分細心地照顧了他幾個小時……直到告別前一刻，他跟我說了很多，他說：「有很多一開始像你一樣的人，但他們從來都不知道自己的錯誤，而你卻意識到自己的不對，你成長了。」隨後他便拿著他的紅白色拐杖離去，只聽見那砰砰的敲擊聲越來越遠，我那慚愧的心也得到了救贖，直到這次活動結束，我才明白當初的我是多麼沒有同理心，對一個無助的失明老人家不但不給予幫助，甚至還戲弄他，現在我才明白「己所不欲，勿施於人」的道理。

在活動結束後，還有一個分享的環節，到我分享時，我說道：「他們雖盲，但心不『盲』。平日裡，我們不應該對他們抱有偏見，應將心比心，推己及人，考慮對方的感受。」台下有人嘲笑，有人嗤之以鼻，我也淡然地笑了笑，笑自己以前的無知和現在的後悔，笑他們又何嘗不是以前那沒有同理心的我的倒影呢？

星期一，同樣是上學，在等紅綠燈時，突然響起那熟悉的敲打聲，回首一望，只見那蒙著黑布，拿著紅白色拐杖的老人家再一次在這出現，看樣子是又在等別人扶他過馬路，這次我沒有嘲笑，沒有偏見，而是去幫助他走過對面。他依舊嗅了我衣服的味道，甚麼都沒有說，我們兩個笑著走到對面，甚麼都沒有說，但卻好像甚麼都說了，因為他需要我作為他的「眼睛」。這時，我才算真正學會代入別人的角度去考慮事情，我也終於學會了「己所不欲，勿施於人」的道理。

「己所不欲，勿施於人」這一句話對於一些人可能還是很模糊，在自己做了別人不喜歡的事卻沒有意識到，在別人做了相同的事在自己身上卻抱怨對方。寫老人被戲耍是想更容易讓人理解這些比較抽象的道理，也可以增加趣味性，讓大家看到筆者從不懂這道理到獲得諒解後的自我救贖過程。希望大家可以及早明白這一道理，不用重蹈「我」的覆轍，可以避免受到良心的譴責。

「那天，我學會甚麼是無常……」

5D 洪紫荊

　　從那天之後，我終於明白了姥姥嘴裏常說的「無常」是甚麼意思。生命的無常讓我們認真地過好每一天；得失的無常讓我們曉得了我們擁有的是多麼來之不易；人與人之間的人際關係無常讓我們重視每一段感情。無常讓我們明白了要珍惜當下時刻，即使是失去了也能坦然面對，因為我們曾擁有過、珍惜過。

　　伴隨這一股股濃郁的消毒水味，醫院裡，嘈雜的聲音響徹著耳朵，有充滿著對世界不公的哭嚎聲，有充滿著對新生兒降生的歡喜雀躍聲。醫院是個神聖的地方，也是令人畏懼的地方。新生在這裡誕生，但也有人在這裡結束了這一生的旅程。

　　午休時被老師告知姥姥突然暈倒了，已送往醫院，如同晴天霹靂般，我馬不停蹄地趕往醫院，我不願相信這個事實，心裡暗自安慰道：姥姥可能是勞累了。我跌跌撞撞地來到醫院，跟著醫生的指示，終於來到了姥姥的病房。「囡囡，你來了。」看到往日不曾常見的父母臉色凝重地站在那裡，我知道我不能再欺騙自己了。看到姥姥像布娃娃般毫無生機地躺在病床上，臉上掛著呼吸機才得以維持生命，心臟像是被無數大手緊捏著，無助和恐慌爭先恐後地蔓延，包圍著我，令我喘不上氣。歲月不知是甚麼時候

帶走了姥姥的年華，在她身上肆無忌憚地繪畫著，畫出一道道痕跡，時間過得真快啊！我踮起腳尖，小心翼翼地、靜悄悄地來到姥姥身旁，俯身靠近姥姥的心臟處，聽見心臟收縮，血液被泵出的「砰砰」聲，我才鬆了一口氣。我反覆確認幾次，仿佛只有這樣才能證明姥姥還在我的身邊。

「姥姥，這是怎麼了？為甚麼會……這嚴重嗎？」我的眼淚再也止不住的往下掉。對於我而言，姥姥佔據了我整個童年，彌補了父母所缺失的愛，給我關懷，尊重和愛。「情況不是很樂觀。」媽媽嘆息道，「為甚麼？分明之前還好好的，而且姥姥答應我要陪我長大，我們要一起度過未來的生活，姥姥她不能食言！」情緒再也無法控制住，如潮水般傾湧而下，我掩著鼻子抽泣。眼淚劃過我的臉頰，在乾燥的皮膚上留下一道道曲折的線痕。我恨，我恨世間為何如此不公；我恨，我恨為甚麼時間要悄然帶走她的年華；而我更恨的是為甚麼發生得這麼突然，我卻做不了甚麼……

車窗的景物快速移動著，回望那條熟悉的道路，那是我與姥姥在無數個日夜牽著手漫步回家的道路。眼前浮現起一幀幀畫面，那是兒時的我被姥姥那雙溫暖且乾燥的手包裹著，彎起她那筆直的腰背，耐心地聽我剛學會說話，含糊不清的話語。隨著車往深處開去，我漸漸地長大了，慢慢地身高超過了姥姥，而姥姥的腰卻不再筆直，昔日的景象倒轉過來，現在的我一手包裹住姥姥那

滿是皺紋、瘦弱的手，聊天時彎下腰去聆聽姥姥的話語，那是兒時一起回家的感覺，仍一樣溫暖著我心頭。

　　四季不知交替了多少次，日與月不知更迭了多少回。那條熟悉的道路彷彿是條時間線，越往裡走，有人在漸漸成長，也有人漸漸老去。不禁感慨，時間真是讓人猝不及防的東西。但人們心中總認為這種變化是常態，繼續追求那種「常」，認為自己能控制一切，沉溺在物慾中，有種種的渴愛和依戀。我們能接受四季變化的無常，但我們重視的人和事呢？

　　終於到家了，我去姥姥房間收拾她的衣物，看著姥姥常坐在那裡等我放學的搖椅，如今停止了搖晃，為我織的毛衣尚未完成，不禁又悲從中來。坐在搖椅上，手裡拿著姥姥平時最喜愛的相機，而相機裡則是她偷拍我的相片，許多張都像是因為心虛怕我發現，畫面模糊得不像話。我不喜歡拍照，也曾制止過姥姥，但相機裡仍有我的新相片，在相中姥姥似乎也想和我同框，每一張裏都能找到她的身影。

　　也許是媽媽知道我沉浸在悲傷中無法自拔，便走了過來，撫摸著我頭，「還在難過嗎？圖圖，你知道人總會有老去的一天。」「我知道，可為甚麼它來的這麼快？這麼突然。突然得我有點反應不過來。姥姥還有三十幾年的光陰呢，為甚麼發生得這麼猝不

及防！」我聲音哽咽地說道。「囡囡啊！我也曾像你這樣不解，甚至是憤怒。你外公在我十八歲的時候，工作期間出現了意外，他甚麼也沒有交代就走了。我曾經也感到束手無策、迷茫。我一直想不通明明有許多的時光，為甚麼就突然終止了。就在我陷入深深不解中的時候，你姥姥來找我談話了，此後我便不再糾結。」話語剛落，她指了指了外面我與姥姥一起種的梨樹，我疑惑地望去，「你看，我們都知道梨樹在秋天的時候，葉子都會全落下，但現在還未到秋天，它也依然落葉。風起葉落，這一些都無跡可循，我們不能提前預知風甚麼時候起，葉甚麼時候落，沒有事物會只按照我們所認知的時間階段發生變化，只是因為適當的條件在因緣配合下才會出現，沒有其必然性。不是人人都能長命百歲，我們最終都會走向死亡。我們無法預知我們會得到甚麼又會失去多少，這一切都太無常了！」「所以這世間有很多事情不是我們能決定的、預知的，發生的一切都是猝不及防。所以這就叫『無常』？」突然靈光乍現，腦海裏呈現了昔日姥姥常掛在嘴邊的「無常」原來是這個意思。「是姥姥常說的『無常』嗎？」媽媽會心一笑：「原來她也跟你說了，我們既然無法預知，我們索性就去接受它，傷心難過是難免，是人之常情，但我們也不能氣餒。與其消極面對一切，不如就珍惜當下的每一分、每一秒，這樣就算再有甚麼意想不到的事發生，我們也不會有遺憾，因為我們曾經擁有過，珍惜過。『無常』能幫助我們放開『常』的執著。」

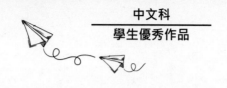

聽完這番話，腦中的霧霾一散而去，隨即帶走的是我的疑惑，不愜。對啊！事物不能時時常態，季季不能如春。萬物皆有自己的定數，只不過是時間的問題。人生起起落落，跌宕起伏，我們沒有預知未來的能力，無法提前知曉結果，不能知道災難與明天哪個會先到來。與其常常懷惶恐之情，害怕未來會發生的事，不如把握當下，將激情投入，隨心所欲，熱灑青春，珍惜當下。畢竟無常才是人生常態。

前往醫院的路上，相比之前的忐忑不安，如今卻多了一絲平靜。手裏捧著姥姥的相機，我想用我的方式去珍惜當下時光，不給自己留下任何遺憾。汽車飛快地行駛著，很快就到了醫院。走進病房，姥姥剛醒，似乎是感受到了我的氣息，目光隨即匯聚在我身上，眼眸似乎多了一道光。「囡囡啊，你來啦！」眼神中透露著除了高興還有一絲其他情緒，我知道，那是姥姥害怕我擔心。我走過去輕輕擁著她說：「姥姥，我們合影一張，好不好？」姥姥似乎也有些詫異，但面對突如其來的請求還是答應了。鏡頭下，我和姥姥彼此依偎在一起，我們彼此相望。快門鍵按下的那瞬間，夕陽沒有了雲的遮蓋，陽光透過窗戶落在了我和姥姥的臉上，我看見了——那是我們之間對彼此的愛。無論事事如何變化，唯一不變的是我們的愛。

花無百日紅，總會凋落；人不會永保青春，總會老去。在時

間的洪流裏，未知的事物實在是太多了，雖然最終我們都會走向死亡，但我們亦有收穫。雖然花失去了它最燦爛的笑顏，然而它在生命消逝前，領略了世間的千姿百態，而它消逝的身軀會由種子延續下去，這是它來過的痕跡。我們不會永保青春，只停留在某個階段。但我們從剛出生的牙牙學語到踏入進二次發育的青少年，再到中年甚至到老年，我們在經歷這些階段時都會有不同的收穫。我們懂得了感恩、體諒、感懷及愛護，這些和我們逝去的生命將在我們的子子孫孫身上傳承下去，而他們會替我們領略這世間的美景，體驗沙子摩擦皮膚的觸感，感受海水湧向腳尖的溫度。

> 成長至此回顧過往，感覺小時候死亡離我們非常遙遠，但隨著我們長大，仿佛「死亡」這個字眼也悄然而來。到處都能聽到身邊人突然離世的消息，無論是意外還是老去，都讓我萬分震驚。那一段時間裡常喃喃自語道：為甚麼？想必大家都有經歷過這種「無常」的變化，無論是感情得失還是生命的流逝。這篇主要是圍繞著外婆寫的，在現實中外婆已經不在世了。記得外婆去世的時候，自己也曾有過難過，也因為未能珍惜外婆在世的時光，心中萬分遺憾。希望這篇文章能彌補自己的遺憾，同時也想告訴大家珍惜當下擁有的一切事物，不留遺憾。

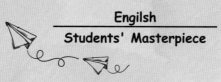
A Restaurant Review

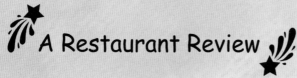

1A   Lee Lok Wang

The restaurant is called $5000 Restaurant. It is in Tin Shui Wai. It opens from 10 am to 4 pm and 6 pm to 11 pm. It serves Chinese food. There are a lot of delicious and tasty dishes served at this restaurant. We can try noodles, fake shark fin soup, spring rolls and fried rice in this restaurant. We can also order desserts.

The restaurant was a brand-new Chinese restaurant. There were some comfortable sofas. It was quiet and was located near the sea. You will be able to view an eye-catching scenery while you enjoy the meal. I liked the funny and cosy decorations. I was glad that I got the chance to dine at this restaurant.

We ordered fake shark fin soup as our main course. It tasted delicious. We also ordered hand-made soup and drinks.

The hand-made soup was creamy. It tasted a lot better than that in other restaurants. However, there was one thing I wanted to criticize - that was the tasteless dessert! The cheesecake was not sweet.

Their service was quite good. The waiter and waitresses were very polite. They gave us some suggestions about the food they served too. The price was cheap. The average price was around HK $30 a person per meal. If you want to try tailor-made food, it may be more expensive. I enjoyed the visit. In short, I would recommend this restaurant to all of you. It is worth trying and it is best for family gatherings. Don't hesitate! Go for it!

> This restaurant review is written by Lee Lok Wang from 1A. He talks about his dining experience after his visit to a Chinese restaurant. He reviews the food, decorations and service of the restaurant. Would you like to give it a try after his recommendation?

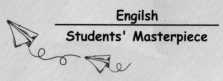

A Self-introduction

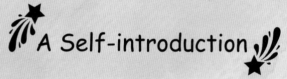

1A Munaf Khainath Bibi

My name is Munaf Khainath Bibi. I am 12 years old. My school's name is Buddhist Mau Fung Memorial College. I am in Class 1A. I have 6 family members. I have two younger brothers and one younger sister. My dad is a FedEx worker. My mom is a housewife. My younger brother is slim and tall. He likes to play with his friends at the park. My other younger brother is short and handsome. My younger sister is short and chubby. Many people think she is cute. I have long, straight hair. I am tall but I am very shy. Some people say that I have a beautiful smile. My favourite food is salad because it is delicious. My favourite idol is Chopin because he inspired me to play the piano. I am still learning how to play it. I want to be a pianist when I grow up. I like reading and drawing, but I don't like doing my homework. My favourite video game is Roblox. My favourite subjects are Math and Music. My favourite colours are red and purple. I am gentle and caring.

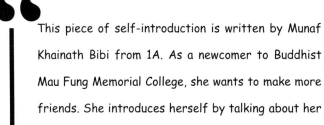

This piece of self-introduction is written by Munaf Khainath Bibi from 1A. As a newcomer to Buddhist Mau Fung Memorial College, she wants to make more friends. She introduces herself by talking about her hobbies, her family, her appearance and her personalities. With her friendly character, it is doubtless that she will have a happy life at school.

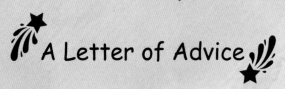

A Letter of Advice

2A Mirza Iman Fiaz

Dear Kitty,

Thanks for your email. I'm sorry to hear about your problems. It sounds like you are having a tough time! Don't worry! Let me give you some advice to solve your problems.

First, you mentioned that there is a lack of space at home. You may feel annoyed or helpless because your home is very noisy. Your parents are always watching TV and your siblings are playing loudly. Let me give you some advice. First, you can ask your parents to lower the volume and ask your siblings to be quiet. Besides, if I were you, I would go to the public library or a friend's house to study. Also, you can stay at school and do all your homework.

Also, you mentioned that there is a lack of communication in your family. You may feel lonely and depressed because your

parents are too busy with work and everyone is glued to his or her phone. Let me give you some advice. First, you can ask your parents to shut off their phones during mealtimes or you can also tell your parents about your feelings. Moreover, you can have more family picnics or outings. Also, I think you can have more FaceTime calls when your parents are not at home.

Moreover, you mentioned that you have money problems because you think you don't have enough pocket money. You may feel annoyed and confused. I think that you have enough pocket money but don't use it in a better way. For example, you often spend too much money on new clothes, new phones and new watches. Let me give you some cool advice. First, you can build up a habit of saving money wisely and don't buy useless stuff, although you can buy useful stuff like pens and notebooks.

Why not follow my advice and give it a try? If you follow my advice, I think things will get better and you'll be happier than before.

Best,

Iman

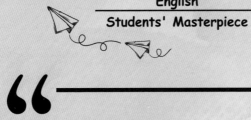
"

This letter is written by Mirza Iman Fiaz from 2A. She tries to offer some advice to her friend who is desperate for help. You can feel her sincerity when you read her letter and she really wants to help her friend walk out from the darkness.

"

The Hong Kong Zoological and Botanical Gardens

2C Lok Cyrus

The Hong Kong Zoological and Botanical Gardens is in Central. You can get there by bus, minibus and Peak Tram. It opens from 5 am to 10 pm. At this park, you can see different kinds of animals and plants.

At the Fountain Terrace Garden, you can see a memorial arch at the entrance. You can get information about the Peak and appreciate the architecture. If you walk to the middle of the garden, you can see a fountain. Also, you can see the beautiful view and take photos of the garden. If you go to the side of the garden, you can see a kiosk and a visitor centre. You can take a break there.

At the Mammal Enclosure and Reptile Exhibit, you can find different animals. If you visit the Mammal Enclosure,

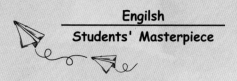
you can see monkeys. Also, you can take photos and videos of them. If you go to the Reptile Enclosure, you can see tortoises. Also, you can know more information about them. They are the largest species of tortoises in the world.

At the Aviary, you can see different kinds of birds, for example, flamingoes and cranes. You can learn more about these birds by reading from the signs.

This park is an excellent place for knowing about animals and plants. You must go there if you have time.

This information leaflet is written by Lok Cyrus from 2C. After his visit to the Hong Kong Zoological and Botanical Gardens, he has written this piece of writing to introduce the place. You can know more about this park after reading his leaflet.

A Postcard to a Friend

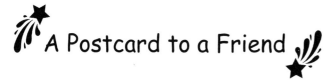

2C Leung Cho Kong

Dear Chris,

How do you do? Peter and I are having a great time in Hong Kong! It's a pity that you cannot come with us. Let me tell you something about our trip.

I am writing this postcard at the hotel that I'm staying. I can't believe my eyes right now. The room is well-decorated and the bed is extremely comfortable. We just came back from shopping at a nearby mall. We've got some gifts that I think you'll like.

Yesterday was a blast! We visited Hong Kong Wetland Park. It's located in Tin Shui Wai. You can take the Light Rail and get off at Wetland Park station. What I'm going to tell you may not sound real. We saw some fish and frogs that are super huge! There were also exotic birds to look at so we brought a pair of binoculars. There were also jumpy fishes which are super funny to just watch them flap and flop. Of course, we saw the most famous crocodile, Pui Pui.

Tomorrow, we'll go to the Peak Tower. It's really far away from where our hotel is, but it'll be worth visiting! I have already seen some photos of the Peak on Instagram and they look so beautiful! I remember that you've been to the wax museum before, right? I just know that it is a good place to take some pictures with the wax models of some celebrities. The more I talk about this, the more excited I get! I hope tomorrow will be awesome.

For sure, we're going to gift you a lot of souvenirs. We can't wait to see your reaction!

Bye for now!

Best wishes,

Ben

This postcard is written by Leung Cho Kong from 2C. He imagines that he comes from another country and writes this postcard to his friend. He gives details of the places that he has been. You can definitely feel his excitement in his writing.

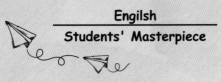
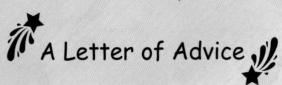

A Letter of Advice

2C Zhang Jing

Dear Kitty,

Thank you for your email. I'm sorry you have a few problems and you don't know what to do. Don't worry I will give you some advice to help you.

First, you mentioned in your email that you have nowhere to study. I know that you feel helpless because there is a lack of space at home. You should go to the library to study. If I were you, I would find a quiet place to study.

Second, you mentioned in your email that your family members don't talk to you. I know that you feel lonely because you have nobody to talk to at home. You should talk to your teachers and social workers about your problems. If I were you, I would try to call my parents more often so that

they can chat with me. It is good to do something together.

Third, you mentioned in your email that you don't have enough pocket money. I know that you feel helpless because you don't have enough money to buy something you like. You should control yourself on spending money. If I were you, I would not buy things I don't need.

Good luck! I'm sure things will get better soon.

Best wishes,

Chris

This letter is written by Zhang Jing from 2C. She tries to help her friend by offering a lot of suggestions. She shows her empathy by putting herself into her friend's shoes. A friend in need is a friend indeed!

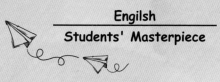

A Charity Day

3B Cheung Kwok Hin

Last week on 18th October, a charity day was held. It was an event to help raise money for the Community Chest. It is a non-profit organisation which provides social services to people in need. As a club member, I was invited to participate in the event.

On that day, a charity sale was organised at the school hall. We collected some old materials from students and teachers such as old school uniforms, second-hand books and laptops. I thought no one wants old things nowadays. However, something unexpected happened. All the second-hand books were sold out in 10 minutes. I was shocked when someone told me the truth.

Jerry bought 500 books. I interviewed him and asked, 'Why do you buy 500 books?' He replied, 'Oh! I have decided

to donate all of them to the children who live in poverty.' He was so generous.

In the afternoon, an obstacle race was organised at the school playground. We prepared some obstacles with different levels of difficulty for both junior and senior form students. Form 1 to Form 3 students participated in the easy level zone to ensure a safe and fun race. Form 4 to Form 6 students participated in the hard level zone because they are physically stronger. One of them said, 'It was really hard but fun. As a Form 3 student, I am interested in trying it. As a result, I was really tired. Although I found this race difficult, I felt I became stronger than before! Haha!'

Overall, that was a day of non-stop fun. I really hope everyone will join the charity day and have fun next year.

"

This school magazine article is written by Cheung Kwok Hin from 3B. He gives a number of details about the event and expresses his feelings as a participant. You can actually feel his enthusiasm for it!

"

A Meaningful Charity Day

3E Chen Hei Yeung

Last weekend, a Charity Day was held on the 10th of October from 1 pm to 5 pm by Buddhist Mau Fung Memorial College Social Services Club. It was an event to help raise money for the Children Cancer Foundation. It is a non-profit making organization which helps children with cancer in Hong Kong. As a club member, I was invited to participate in the event.

On this day, the first fundraising event was a talent show which was held at the school hall from 1 pm to 2 pm. It was an amazing show. There were many performances, for example, singing, dancing and magic. Eventually, in the talent show, $1500 was raised and we felt very satisfied.

The second activity was a charity sale which was held at the school playground from 2 pm to 3 pm. This activity let

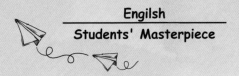
people sell things which they no longer needed. Someone made their own biscuits too on that day. Eventually, in the charity sale, $700 was raised and we felt so satisfied.

The last fundraising event was having booth games. The booth games were held at the playground from 3 pm to 5 pm. We sold tickets to participants. They bought tickets as donations and they could play the games. Many families joined us. Finally, $2600 was raised and which was used to help people in need.

It was a fun day! The best thing is that it was all for a good cause! Over $4800 was raised. I really hope everyone gets involved in the charity day next year.

This school magazine article is written by Chen Hei Yung from 3E. It mainly reports the activities held on a Charity Day. From his writing, you get to know more about the details of the event and how successful it is.

A Letter of Advice

4A Huang Ho Yee

Dear Taylor,

How have you been? I'm busy with my schoolwork. I hope you're getting on all right. I was sorry to hear of your worries about the coming job interview. Don't worry! I'm sure the following advice can help you a lot!

The first thing you have to bear in mind is to prepare well for the interview. I suggest you can obtain information from websites in order to know the job duties and job requirements. Being a tutor, you need to teach your students patiently. They may not understand what you say, so you need to explain very clearly. Also, you need to understand your students' emotions. Sometimes, you need to talk to them to solve their puzzles. Furthermore, you need to handle parents' enquiries. If parents find you, you have to answer them

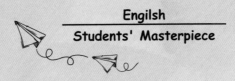

appropriately. You can search for the job requirements on websites. First, you should have a good command of Chinese and English. If you were poor in Chinese or English, how would you teach your students well? Also, you should have knowledge of reading and writing in Chinese and English. If you are weak in languages, you cannot teach them. Furthermore, you should have basic computer skills. If you don't have basic computer skills, you cannot even type teaching materials to your students. Thus, it is perfectly clear that you have to prepare well in order to get the job.

The second thing you have to bear in mind is to prepare what to do during the interview. Before the interview, you have to keep your hair tidy and clean. If your hair were not tidy, how would you impress your interviewer? Also, you need to trim your nails. This can show your politeness during your interview. Furthermore, you need to wear tidy and proper clothing. With appropriate clothing, I'm sure your interviewer will be impressed by your handsome look! During the interview, you have to maintain eye contact and wear a smile. You can show your confidence to the interviewer. Also, you have to sit up straight. This can show your sincerity and seriousness during the interview. Thus, it is perfectly clear that you have to prepare for the interview in order to get the job.

I hope my advice would help you with your problem. I think I have to go now and attend to my homework. Keep me posted on your progress

Yours,

Chris Wong

This letter is written by Huang Ho Yee from 4A. She tries to help her friend overcome her anxiety about having a job interview by offering some useful advice. You can also learn some useful tips about what to do before the interview and during the interview.

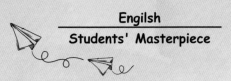

Experience Sharing of Being a Waiter

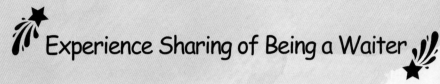

4B Chan Tsz Wai

The best part of my job

I am a waiter who works at Tai Hing, a chain restaurant providing a variety of cuisines. Many people may think that this job can be very stressful and tiring. However, if you think my job is tedious and physically demanding, then you are nowhere to be correct. One of the best parts of being a waiter is when serving the meals to diners and seeing them smile back at me, as well as complimenting my service with a "thank you". These things do in fact motivate me to carry on my career despite fatigue and boredom in my work.

The biggest challenge I have ever faced in my job

Being a waiter, it is inevitable for you to encounter rude customers. However, there was once a middle-aged man who really irritated me. He literally complained about every flaw of the restaurant. I was getting angry, and I was about to

fight back. But I told myself to keep cool and bear with patience and endurance. Once my boss came, he banned him from the restaurant. 'Thank god, I don't have to face him again.' I murmured to myself. I said thank you to him, but he apologized for what I needed to go through.

My most memorable moment

Everyone has a memorable, unforgettable moment in their lifetime and will cherish those memories as long as they live. I am one of those many people with a memorable moment in my job. Stephen Chow Sing-chi, who is a very famous celebrity in Hong Kong, randomly came to our restaurant. Surprisingly, the manager put me in charge to serve this noteworthy man. I started to be nervous when I approached him. I could remember each sweat that was dripping down my body. I was keeping my lips tight. However, when I realized that I should not have this feeling, I should have thought of him as a normal customer. And thus, it was a success. Stephen even complimented me for being such a wonderful waiter. If I had never met Stephen in my work, I don't think I would've improved my services.

"This piece of sharing is written by Julian Chan Tsz Wai from 4B. He imagines that he works in a restaurant as a waiter and shares the best part of his job, his challenges and his most memorable moment. He includes some interesting and creative ideas in his writing. Let's find out more by reading his writing."

My Views on Building a New Amusement Park in Hong Kong

5D Lau Ka Ying

Dear Editor,

With just a few clicks on the keyboard and the mouse, you will see articles about suggestions on building a new amusement park flooding your news feed. It is recommended that the government should build a theme park about dinosaurs.

First of all, Hong Kong Disneyland and Ocean Park have a long history. They are the most popular theme parks among Hong Kong people but under the current situation, many people have chosen not to visit these two theme parks. Also, we know that they do not have new facilities and it is more difficult to attract people to visit them. As a result, we definitely need a new amusement park. Ocean Park is about

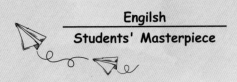

animals and Disneyland is about cartoon characters. These theme parks are very common in other countries. However, we do not see a theme park about dinosaurs around the globe. It is a good idea to build one. If there is an amusement park about dinosaurs, attractions like taking photos with AI dinosaurs can't be missed.

Visitors can take photos with their favourite AI dinosaurs. For instance, Tyrannosaurus, Triceratops, Spinosaurus, Allosaurus, Xillong, Diplodocus and so on. The above dinosaurs are very famous representative species. Also, children can go on rides about dinosaurs. Second, they could have a safari tour to see different kinds of dinosaurs. They can get a closer look at dinosaurs in their real sizes. Moreover, there could be a museum to talk about dinosaurs' history and culture in order to enable tourists to know more about dinosaurs.

Building a new amusement park will bring us benefits. If there is a new amusement park, it will attract more visitors

to come to Hong Kong. Hong Kong has never had any big zoos, so we need to go to other countries to see animals, like giraffes, chimpanzees and so on. If we have a dinosaur theme park in Hong Kong, it will attract more visitors. Also, children can learn more about the famous species of dinosaurs. Dinosaurs have already been extinct for millions of years. They cannot be seen anywhere. Having a dinosaur theme park in Hong Kong can attract foreign tourists to spend time and money here. Moreover, a new amusement park can create job opportunities, many people have lost their jobs during the epidemic. If we build a dinosaur theme park, we can provide some jobs to the unemployed, for instance, tour guides, staff members, controllers, conductors and cleaners and so on. These jobs are important in a theme park.

Taking all aspects into account, building a new amusement park about dinosaurs can be considered.

Yours faithfully,
Chris Chan

"

The letter to the editor is written by Lau Ka Ying from 5D. In the letter, she expresses her urge to have a dinosaur theme park as the third amusement park in Hong Kong. She has also given some innovative ideas about the attractions to be included. If you had a chance, would you like to visit her dream park?

"

The Pros and Cons of Undergoing Plastic Surgery

5D Li Ka Ying

Why has cosmetic surgery become so popular nowadays? There are different reasons why cosmetic surgery has become so popular nowadays. Many people are influenced by Korean culture which embraces technological advances and they would like to pursue outer beauty. The advanced technology makes cosmetic surgery less risky and contributes to faster recovery time. Also, cosmetic surgery can boost mental health. That's why cosmetic surgery has become so popular nowadays.

There are many advantages of cosmetic surgery. First, cosmetic surgery can improve people's mental health. People who get plastic surgery see a lift in their emotional state. While beauty may be on the surface, self-image is deeply tied to a person's emotional well-being. Whether you are getting a facelift to get your groove back or having reconstructive surgery to become a whole new you, cosmetic surgery can open the door to a happier, healthier life. When you feel good about yourself, you have less anxiety about social interactions. With less anxiety, your social life can blossom. You might find yourself with a renewed desire to try new foods or new fashions. Imagine living with less stress and more friends, it can improve your mental health. Another advantage of cosmetic surgery procedure is that in some cases it can enhance your physical health. For example, a rhinoplasty surgery not only will enhance the look and shape of your nose but may also help with respiratory issues that you may have.

However, there are many disadvantages of cosmetic surgery. First, there could be adverse effects on your body. This will make your physical condition worse than before. Second, cosmetic surgery is costly. This is because the cost of cosmetic surgery is very high, it will waste a lot of your money, resulting in an increase in your financial burden. This factor makes cosmetic surgery not so 'easily accessible' to everyone, as it can be difficult saving up money for cosmetic surgeries, so people may take loans, which can lead to debts. Therefore, people will be anxious about returning the money to loan companies. Third, people may become addicted to cosmetic surgery. Since people may not feel satisfied after the surgery and want to pursue a better appearance, they may want to have cosmetic surgery again. People will easily get addicted to cosmetic surgery as they will never be satisfied with their looks. Fourth, cosmetic surgery can go wrong. For example, a facelift can cause permanent nerve damage which leads to facial paralysis. This is undoubtedly a devastating outcome, which should be taken into consideration. In extreme cases, these mistakes are irreversible and cannot be fixed.

To conclude, there are both advantages and disadvantages for cosmetic surgery. Therefore, people should pay more attention to the risks before making the decision.

This essay is written by Li Ka Ying from 5D. In her essay, she tries to analyse both the pros and cons of undergoing cosmetic surgery and tells the readers to think carefully before making such an important decision.

樂韻賢聚

古箏演奏：梁子可 2C

演奏曲目：戰颱風

簡介：《戰颱風》由著名古箏演奏家王昌元於六十年代創作，樂曲表現了碼頭工人頑強不屈的精神。梁子可同學在古箏方面表現出色，多次榮獲本港以至大灣區的多項大獎，她亦獲邀於中央電視台高清綜藝娛樂頻道的藝術推廣節目《花開盛世》中表演，最近亦於勵志協進會及香港金域假日酒店的兒童慈善時裝秀中演奏古箏，充分展現出她音樂才華。

古箏演奏：梁子可2C

演奏曲目：瑤族舞曲

簡介：《瑤族舞曲》由劉鐵山、茅沅創作，作曲家運用管弦樂的手法，豐富地展現瑤族民眾歡歌熱舞的喜慶場面。梁子可同學手法嫻熟，技術精湛，將此曲特點發揮得淋漓盡致。

樂韻賢聚

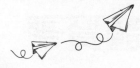

鋼琴演奏：葉梓芊6D

演奏曲目：The Maiden's Prayer, Op. 4

簡介：《少女的祈禱》（The Maiden's Prayer, Op. 4），是波蘭女作曲家特克拉·巴達捷夫斯卡--巴拉諾夫斯卡的傳世名作。葉梓芊同學獲英國皇家音樂學院聯合委員會六級鋼琴演奏考試優異、五級樂理優異，現為鋼琴七級水平，並於香港學校音樂節鋼琴演奏取得優良成績。

小提琴演奏：沈奧翔5A

演奏曲目：Canon in D major

簡介：《D大調卡農》（Canon in D major）是巴洛克時期德國作曲家約翰·帕海貝爾最著名的作品。沈奧翔同學於香港學校音樂節鋼琴演奏取得優良成績，並常於校內大型活動進行表演，備受讚賞，現為小提琴八級水平。

樂韻賢聚

步操管樂團：

鄭悅強2A、張灝2B、黃傲勤2B、溫諾言2C、吳巧恩2D、

陳樂兒3A、鄭添翔3A、施恩榮3A、張玥婷3A、黃景星3B、

許子樂3D、余家熙3D、陳治國3D、馬文傑3D、謝思藝3E、

陳薁名4A、劉晉廷4A、孫甲章4A、李文樂4A、凌楚蕎4C、

梁耀朗4D、吳貽焜4D、李聖瑩4E、朱宣蓓4E、許子謙4E

演奏曲目：Scotland the brave；Ode to joy；Mickey mouse

簡介：本校步操管樂團成立於 1999 年，目的為培養學生對音樂的興趣、管樂器和敲擊樂器的訓練以及提供紀律的訓練，樂團成立至今經常代表學校出席表演活動。樂團於香港步操及鼓號樂團協會舉辦的香港步操樂團公開賽獲得銀獎，更獲北京市旅遊局邀請，參加「北京國際旅遊節」表演及獲發優秀表現獎。

樂韻賢聚

中國鼓隊：

徐彩瀅2D、馮永雯2D、鄭添翔3A、王凱怡3A、張玥婷3A、
陳卓權3D、張孝南3D、劉思琪3D、王曉峰3D、余家熙3D、
許子謙4E

表演曲目：香港活力鼓令廿四式

簡介：本校中國鼓隊旨在讓學生認識中國音樂文化，透過訓
練培養學生自律、表達、專注及協調能力，實現團隊精神。
鼓隊於香港中樂團香港鼓樂節20周年2023「香港活力鼓令24
式」擂台賽，表現優秀，備受讚許。

馮凱琳 (1D)
奇異的動物（繪畫）

馮永雯 (1D)
奇異的動物（繪畫）

黃淑真 (1D)
奇異的動物（繪畫）

陳盈茵 (1D)
奇異的動物（繪畫）

以點、線、面為創作元素，加入豐富想像力，繪畫一幅獨一無二的畫作。

陳柏爾 (1B)
正立方體素描

馮永雯 (1D)
正立方體素描

文依敏 (2A)
球體素描

陳家琳 (2D)
球體素描

殷宏富 (3A)

我的自畫像（素描）

李聖瑩 (3C)

我的自畫像（素描）

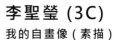

陳熹洋 (3E)

我的自畫像（素描）

鄧葆賢 (3E)

我的自畫像（素描）

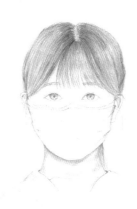

鄧嘉雯 (4A)
靜物素描

鄧嘉雯 (4A)
風景畫（素描）

林傲妍 (4D)
風景畫（素描）

吳嘉璇 (4D)
風景畫（素描）

戚凱怡 (1A)
昆蟲樂園（版畫）

馮永雯 (1D)
昆蟲樂園（版畫）

以「昆蟲樂園」為主題，創作一幅單色紙版畫。

劉創棋 (3B)
我的肖像（版畫）

譚鍵烽 (3E)
我的肖像（版畫）

以「我的肖像」為主題，創作一幅單色凸版畫。

陳敏蓁 (2B)
約定極光（繪畫）

曾明鋒 (2D)
約定極光（繪畫）

美莎 (2C)
約定極光（繪畫）

陸宇鵬 (2D)
約定極光（繪畫）

毛雅汶 (2C)
約定極光（繪畫）

梁芸曦 (2D)
約定極光（繪畫）

以鄰近色及明度色彩原理，繪畫極光效果作為背景。加入人、動物或大自然剪影圖像，展現出在神秘極光下的活動情境。

鄭添翔 (2A)
扇面水墨畫

張聖欣 (2B)
扇面水墨畫

梁芷琪 (2B)
扇面水墨畫

陳治國 (2D)
扇面水墨畫

以白描技法，臨摹一幅以花卉／植物／動物為題材的絹面水墨畫。

殷宏富 (3A)

當凱斯哈林遇上蒙特里安（繪畫）

林傲蕎 (3E)

當凱斯哈林遇上蒙特里安（繪畫）

李臻希 (3C)

當凱斯哈林遇上蒙特里安（繪畫）

梁倩綾 (3E)

當凱斯哈林遇上蒙特里安（繪畫）

　　學習凱斯哈林及蒙特里安兩位藝術大師的藝術風格，創作一個創意十足的兩點透視魔方。

趙韻姿 (4B)

鸚鵡（彩色鉛筆）

陳朗晴 (4B)

花卉（水彩）

吳雅芝 (4C)

花卉（水彩）

吳嘉璇 (4D)

花卉（水彩）

馮永清 (6A)
突破（陶藝）

面對未知的未來，興奮又害怕。我要蛻變成蝴蝶，突破束縛，重新出發。

鍾音音 (6A)
自由飛翔（陶藝）

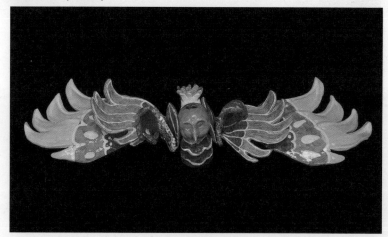

鳥無翅膀不能自由飛翔。擺脫歧視，脫變成長。振翅高飛，走出舒適區，邁進新世界。

嚴姍 (6D)
記憶（陶藝）

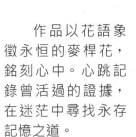

作品以花語象徵永恒的麥稈花，銘刻心中。心跳記錄曾活過的證據，在迷茫中尋找永存記憶之道。

鍾嘉琳 (6B)
Escape(逃)（陶藝）

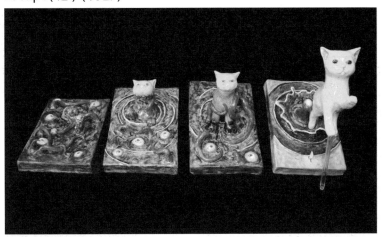

作品以貓代表自己逃出困境。以四塊陶泥磚上長滿藤蔓，眼睛象徵著束縛、限制及不被理解，「貓」努力掙扎，逐漸成長，最終能夠擺脫所有束縛，全身成功逃出。

莫若希 (6B)
重生 (陶藝)

　　受傷及已逝世的動物躺在乾地上，中央湧現火焰團，象徵重生希望。動物攀上火焰，奔向心臟形狀的大自然。心臟象徵生命力，給予大自然重生力量，希望大自然不受人類干擾，永續下去。

黃嘉婧 (6D)
你看到了什麼？(陶藝)

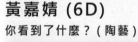

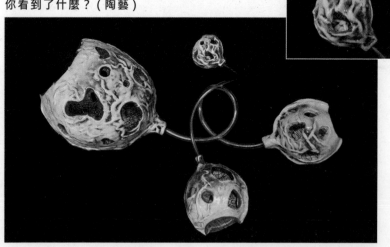

　　眼球內布滿標纖標貼，暗示無意識的話語及偏見。眼球內的白人小人代表「我」，我被別人的目光及標籤禁錮著。